The Purple Heart

The Purple Heart

Barbara Haley

Christian Focus Publications

ISBN 1-85792-920-9

Published by
Christian Focus Publications Ltd,
Geanies House, Fearn, Tain, Ross-shire,
IV20 1TW, Scotland, Great Britain

www.christianfocus.com
email: info@christianfocus.com

Cover design by Alister Macinnes
Cover illustration by Debbie Clark

Printed and bound in Great Britain by
Cox and Wyman Ltd, Reading, Berks.

*As this story is set in America, American spelling
has been used throughout this book.*

I want to say thanks to a special group of fourth graders who begged me to write this book for them. Thanks for your encouragement and prayers – and thanks for laughing in all the right places! I will always love you.

Kayla, Amaris, Sarah, Brianna, Christine, Zoe, Samantha, Jackie, Lauren, Roxanna, Ferris, Maddie, Brittney, Sammy, Michael, Josiah, Ryan, Daniel, Mitchell, and Josh.

Barbara Haley

I want to say thanks to a special group
of fourth graders who helped me to
write this book for them. Thanks for
your encouragement and prayers - and
Thanks for keeping in all the right
places. I will always love you.

Austin, Aaron, Sarah, Briana,
Christine, Zoe, Samantha, Dacus,
Lauren, Alexandra, aria, Maddie,
Bridey, Serena, Michael, Joshua, sa-
Ryan, David, Mitchell, and Josh.

Richard Hazelton

Contents

Contents

My Dad's
A War Hero

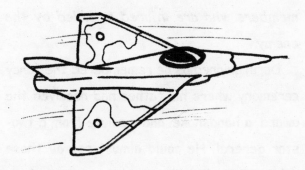

Darin Johnson, a fifth-grader at Freeburg
Elementary School, walked to his locker and
unzipped the pocket in his backpack where he
had stashed his father's gold medal. As he did,
he rehearsed his oral report in his mind.

*My father was injured during the Gulf War.
The enemy bombed a jet he was working on,
and as the plane went up in flames, he crawled
underneath to rescue another soldier who had
been knocked unconscious. A burning pipe fell
from the belly of the plane and landed on my*

9

dad's leg, but he shoved it away and dragged the other man to safety just before the plane exploded. This medal – a Purple Heart – is a special medal given only to American military members who are injured or killed by the enemy.

Darin grinned as he remembered the fancy ceremony where his father had received the award, a handshake, and a salute from a two-star general. He could almost see all those soldiers standing like statues in honor of his dad while the band played 'I'm Glad to Be an American' and the decoration bearer marched up the aisle with the medal on a purple pillow, his eyes staring straight ahead like a zombie. 'Eat your heart out, Andrew. Hannah is going to love my report.' Darin's proud smile faded, along with his daydreams however, when he looked inside his backpack. His face went white and he started to shake. It wasn't there. He yanked everything out – baseball cards, a picture of his dog, and a crumpled dollar bill. It was no use. The medal was not there.

'Oh, God,' he prayed silently, as he shoved his things back in his backpack. 'What am I going to do now? My dad specifically said not to take the medal to school.' Darin thought about his father's scarred right hand and the fact that he would walk with a limp for the rest of his life.

'You may be sure that your sin will find you out,' Numbers 32:23. Darin wished his Sunday school verse hadn't popped into his mind. 'This is one time I hope the Bible is wrong,' he thought to himself – knowing that could never be true.

'Darin,' his teacher called. 'Please go to your seat.'

'Yes, ma'am,' he answered, sliding into his chair. He looked to the front of the room where his best friend, Andrew McGinnis, sat, holding his latest swimming trophy and grinning like he'd just won the lottery. Darin felt something crawling in his stomach and thought he was going to be sick. He took a couple of deep breaths and rubbed his forehead. 'This can't be happening,' he thought.

'You okay, Darin?' It was Hannah Carrico. She sat across from him.

'I don't feel so well,' Darin whispered. His father's words pounded in his ears. 'I'll be glad to bring it for you to show, but I'd rather not take a chance on you having it at school all day.'

Darin fought to keep from crying. How could his father ever understand – let alone forgive him? Why hadn't he respected his father's wishes? 'Oh, God,' he prayed again. 'Please forgive me and help me find Dad's medal before he discovers it is missing.' Darin knew that he was forgiven immediately, but he also knew that God would most likely allow him to suffer consequences in order to learn a lesson.

While his classmates gave their reports, Darin thought about the day before. It had started out quite well. Miss Poe, Darin's teacher, had made an announcement in the morning...

* * *

'Boys and girls,' she said, sticking her pencil behind her ear. 'As I told you on Monday, Mr Trelunki asked each teacher to choose one student for the student council.'

Darin put his pencil down and sat up straight. He knew he had a chance.

His grades were high and he had been elected class president for three years straight. 'Please help me get it,' he prayed silently.

Hannah smiled and Darin smiled back, remembering when the guys teased him for liking her the year before. But not this year. Somehow, the fifth grade boys agreed, the girls had gotten better looking and now acted more like human beings. Besides, some of the girls made them feel all funny inside – a good kind of funny. Hannah was cute – there was no question about that. Andrew thought so, too, for that matter. Darin loved to see Hannah's dimples when she laughed, and she wore the coolest clothes in the school. But it was more than that. Darin thought about the first day of school when the guys were making fun of Elliot for his new glasses. Hannah had stepped in and taken Elliot's arm. 'I think the glasses make you look intelligent,' she had said. Darin chuckled inside when he remembered the shocked looks on the guys' faces. Then, the next day, when Carolyn lost her lunch money, Hannah had offered to pray for her right in front of everyone. And ten minutes later, Carolyn found the money under her books. Everyone knew Hannah was a Christian, and no one ever made fun of her.

'I try to be good,' Darin thought. He'd gone to church since he was a baby. But he didn't know how to tell others what he believed. Like the day before. At recess, Darin had walked up to a few of his friends who were hooting and laughing like a bunch of cowboys.

'What's so funny,' Darin asked.

'Oh, nothing,' a guy named Mac said. 'You wouldn't get it, anyway. You're a church boy.' Mac raised his eyebrows and elbowed one of the other boys, and they all cracked up again.

Darin had walked away, embarrassed. He really didn't care what they were laughing about. It was probably a dirty joke. But he couldn't help feeling bad because he never witnessed to his friends. When Andrew saw what had happened, he tried to console Darin.

'I feel sorry for you, Darin. Your parents make you go to church, and then all the guys think you're like this perfect person who doesn't want to have fun or anything.'

'Yeah,' Darin said. 'Man,' he had thought, 'I'm such a chicken. I can't even tell Andrew that I go to church because I love God – not just because my parents make me.'

Darin looked over at Hannah, and his smile returned. She would make a great member of the student council.

'That would be okay, too, Lord,' he added to his prayer.

Miss Poe pulled a sealed envelope from behind her back. 'Drum roll, please,' she ordered. The students laughed – like this was an Oscar award or something. Miss Poe was always making school fun.

Slitting the envelope with a silver letter opener, she pulled out a slip of paper and looked up at the class. 'The person I have chosen sets an excellent example in all areas, but especially in the areas of honesty and integrity. I totally trust this student to tell the truth no matter what the situation.'

Andrew looked back from his front row seat and gave Darin a thumbs-up. Embarrassed, Darin motioned for Andrew to turn around. Andrew was a ton of fun, but sometimes he didn't think much before he did stuff. His pranks had gotten him into hot water more than once. Miss Poe took another look at the slip of paper. Like she didn't know what it said.

'This year's representative is. . .' Miss Poe paused and grinned.

'Read it!' the class cheered. Darin could feel his knees shaking.

'This year's winner is Darin Johnson!'

* * *

Later that morning, Miss Poe was teaching maths when there was a loud knock and the classroom door swung open.

'Miss Poe?' It was Mr Trelunki, the principal. In he walked, followed by a huge boy who looked every bit as tall as Miss Poe. The boy's hair was long and hung in his eyes. His faded pants were torn and mended, but clean.

Darin figured that it was the boy's father who came next. Talk about tall – the guy's head practically scraped the top of the doorway. When he passed Darin's desk, he belched. Darin was sure he smelled beer but Miss Poe said nothing and smiled politely.

Andrew must have heard it too because he turned around and rolled his eyes. The students fought hard not to laugh, but a few giggles escaped. Not for long, though. All got quiet immediately when Mr Trelunki scrunched his eyebrows and gave them that 'Straighten up!' look.

Well, it turned out that this kid's father was a first cousin of Mr Trelunki. I guess that would make the kid Mr Trelunki's second cousin. They sure didn't look alike, though.

'Class,' Miss Poe said. 'This is Judd Becker.'

'Hello, Judd,' came the reply in unison.

Judd looked at the floor and shuffled his feet a little.

Darin jumped when Judd's father slapped his son on the back and said, 'Don't be bashful, boy. Tell the nice students hello.'

Judd muttered a quick hello, more like a grunt, actually.

'Come on in, Judd,' Miss Poe said as she led him to the only empty desk in the room. You guessed it. Right behind Darin.

Darin took another look at Mr Becker and

instantly felt sorry for Judd. He remembered his soccer banquet the week before when his own dad kept telling corny jokes and trying to be cool with his friends. 'Man,' he thought, 'my dad has his moments, but he's nothing compared to this guy.'

Turning around to be friendly, Darin realized how huge Judd really was. Darin was used to being teased about being small, but suddenly, Judd's size scared him.

'Judd,' Miss Poe said. 'This is Darin Johnson. I'm sure you two will be good friends.'

Darin smiled, but Judd didn't notice. He was busy gazing into Miss Poe's eyes while flashing a wide smile.

'Oh, charming,' Darin thought. No telling what Miss Poe thought. She quickly turned and scurried to the front of the room.

'Judd will be fine,' she told his father and Mr Trelunki.

Mr Becker chuckled and shook Miss Poe's hand - way too hard. 'If he gives you any trouble, ma'am, you just let me know. 'Course the boy'll probably have to stand to do his work the next day.' Then Mr Becker laughed right out loud and slapped Mr Trelunki on the back. 'Bet you wish more parents were like me, don't you, Ralphie?'

Mr Trelunki got red and looked away. 'We should be going,' he said.

Miss Poe fidgeted a bit at her desk after the men left. Nobody said much. They just watched Miss Poe and waited. Eventually, she regained her composure and gave the maths assignment.

As she began to write problems on the board, Darin turned to offer Judd a piece of paper and a pencil.

But Judd curled his upper lip and snarled. 'Turn around, Tiny! I don't need the likes of you to take care of me.' Then he reached across the aisle and grabbed Hannah's things.

Darin clenched his fists as he swivelled around to face the front. 'You big ox. You really think you're something special!'

Miss Poe missed it all. Darin could feel his ears heating up, and he let out a startled yelp when Judd crammed the end of a pencil into his back and snickered.

Miss Poe turned. 'Something wrong?' Not knowing exactly who had cried out, she looked across the class.

Judd cleared his throat. Darin kept his eyes on his desk and grimaced when Judd spoke out loudly. 'I think everything is fine, now, Miss Poe. Right, Darin?'

Darin looked up and nodded to Miss Poe. Inside, though, everything definitely was not fine. Darin was as mad as a kid who just found out he had to miss his final ball game for his sister's dance recital.

He's A Big Trouble-maker!

On the way to the playground, Andrew hurried to walk alongside Darin. 'What are you going to do?' he asked.

Darin shrugged his shoulders and kicked a rock across the walk. 'I don't know.' But in his mind, Darin was already doing something. He took a deep breath and let it out. 'I guess I'll pray about it. God always helps me with my problems when I do that.'

'You mean you really believe all that stuff about church and God and everything?'

Darin relaxed and laughed. 'Sure, Andrew. Hey – maybe you can come with me to church sometime. It's pretty neat.'

Andrew rolled his eyes and ran off. 'Whatever,' he called back over his shoulder. The boys joined a bunch of younger students already in the middle of a soccer game. Darin played hard, trying to forget his problems. But, as the game slowed down, he noticed Judd walking around the playground all by himself. Darin could tell Judd had his eye on the game, even though he looked in the opposite direction when Darin caught his eyes.

'Hey, Judd,' Darin hollered, without stopping to think. 'Want to play?'

'Are you nuts?' Andrew asked, running up and panting to catch his breath. Kicking the ball to Darin, he added, 'You know you're just asking for trouble.'

'Maybe so,' Darin answered. 'But he looks so lonely. I kind of feel sorry for him.'

Andrew shook his head and started to walk

away. 'You've lost it, Darin. I mean it. You've really lost it!'

Judd rambled across the field until he stood across from Darin. When the younger students saw Judd's size, they stopped in their tracks – like when someone blows the whistle in freeze tag. Darin's classmates backed away quickly.

Judd kicked the ball out from under Darin's foot and shoved him to the ground. 'Who needs your invitation to play, Tiny?' Judd asked. 'Why don't you go play with the girls? They're more your size.'

'Hey!' Andrew shouted. 'Who made you the boss, Judd? Why don't you leave? We were playing here first.'

Darin staggered to his feet, wiping grass from his mouth.

'Yeah,' someone else yelled. 'Who do you think you are? We'll just quit if you play.'

Judd grabbed Darin and twisted his arm behind his back. 'You quit and I'll bust his nose,'

Judd sneered. He kicked the ball across the field. 'Now start playing, you wimps!'

Suddenly a whistle blew. It was Miss Poe. She was pointing and motioning for Judd and Darin to come over to her.

Darin wished he could curl up and crawl away. 'I can't believe this,' he thought. 'I've never been in trouble at school. This creep decides to pick on me and now I'm gonna get yelled at, too. And he's the principal's cousin!' Darin knew his ears were red again, but frankly, he didn't care. Anger whirled inside him like dust on a windy day.

'What's going on, boys?' Miss Poe asked, her hands on her hips.

That's all it took. Darin opened his mouth and began to explain everything. The paper for maths, the pencil in his back, the trouble on the soccer field. Words tumbled out faster than he could think, and before he knew it, he was screaming, and Miss Poe blew the whistle again.

'Darin Johnson,' she scolded. 'You will not talk to me with such disrespect.'

'But you don't understand! He...'

'Darin!' Miss Poe repeated, putting her hand on his shoulder.

Darin looked at his feet and whispered, 'I'm sorry, Miss Poe.' It was all he could do to keep the stinging tears from falling down his face. Wouldn't Judd love that!

'Miss Poe,' Judd said. 'I'm sorry, too, but I think it looked worse than it was. Actually, Darin simply tripped over my foot as we both went for the ball. I admit – we were probably playing too rough. We'll try to do better, right Darin?' Judd slapped Darin on the back gently and smiled. Darin didn't answer.

Miss Poe just stood there staring at them for a few seconds. Then she suggested the boys figure out how to play fairly because recess was almost over.

'Yes, ma'am,' Judd said, as he ran back to the soccer field.

Darin lost it. 'Judd is lying!' he screamed. 'Don't believe him, Miss Poe. He's nothing but a big trouble-maker.'

Miss Poe cleared her throat, and Darin realized he was yelling again.

'I think you need to go have a seat on the bench and cool down, Darin. I'm not sure what's really going on, but your behavior shocks me.'

Darin stormed across the concrete playground and sat down. Hannah was jumping rope nearby. She came and sat down next to him.

'Judd's mean,' she said. 'Did you tell Miss Poe what he did to you?'

Darin shook his head. 'I tried, but I don't think she listened.'

Hannah nodded. 'I hope it's okay,' she murmured. 'I'm praying for you, Darin.'

Unexpected heat rushed to Darin's face. He knew his ears were glowing. 'Thanks, Hannah. I know that will help.'

It's A Genuine
Purple Heart!

Darin was not feeling well when he woke up the next morning. He had dreamed of Judd all night long and was exhausted from dodging punches and running for safety.

He was just about to holler and ask his mother about skipping school when he remembered the oral reports. Andrew had claimed his report would be the best in class. He even hinted that Hannah would like his better than Darin's. Darin couldn't stay home.

He jumped out of bed and threw on his

clothes. As he ran a brush through his hair, he realized that he'd forgotten to ask his father about takiing the medal to school. Leaping down the stairs, two at a time, Darin caught his father just as he was walking out the front door.

Darin begged his father to let him take the purple heart. After a few minutes, though, his father looked at his watch impatiently.

'No, Darin. I'm not at all comfortable with you taking the medal to school. I'm sorry, but it's just too valuable to me. Today won't work, but I could bring it to your classroom on my lunch hour tomorrow. Do you think Miss Poe would agree to that?'

Darin dropped his eyes and managed to produce a few tears. They worked sometimes. 'That's okay, Dad. I know you're busy. I can find something else to talk about.'

'I'm really sorry, Darin. If there were any way I could make it, I would.'

'He's not budging an inch! What am I going

to do?' Darin tried to think of a comeback, but his dad was out the door and in his car before Darin could say a word. 'Great!' he muttered, dragging his feet up the stairs.

* * *

Twenty minutes later, Darin groaned as he pushed his way to the back of the school bus. The only seat left was directly across from Judd. 'With any luck, he won't notice I'm here,' Darin thought. He plopped down in the empty seat and pulled out a comic book to hide behind. But it didn't work.

'Hey, pimple face!' Judd shouted. Roars of laughter exploded from the children nearby. When Darin didn't look up, Judd slapped the comic book from his hands. 'Don't ignore me,' he growled. 'You know better than that.'

Darin picked his comic book up from the floor and said nothing.

'Turn around and mind your own business, Judd.' This came from somewhere in the front of the bus. Darin cringed when he recognized the voice of his 14-year-old sister, Tamara.

'Like you're going to make me?' Judd answered. 'Who are you – his babysitter?' Judd grabbed the comic book and snorted. 'Hey, everybody, there's a picture of the kid on here.' Judd waved the comic around, showing the cover picture. It was a monster with one gigantic eye in the middle of its head. Darin tried to snatch the comic back, but lost his balance and fell off his seat into the aisle.

'Get back in your seat, Darin!' the bus driver screamed.

Judd was almost purple because he was laughing so hard. 'Here, Tiny,' he said, as he offered Darin his hand. 'Let me help you.'

Darin shoved Judd's hand away and climbed back onto his seat. Fortunately, Judd started reading the comic book. Darin didn't even care if he got it back. He was just glad that Judd stayed busy the rest of the way to school.

In the classroom, Darin unpacked his books and things. Andrew was hanging up his jacket nearby and asked, 'What did you bring to show for your report?' Darin motioned for Andrew to come close and unzipped the secret pocket inside his backpack. Holding it open only enough for his friend to see, Darin picked up the golden medal and pulled it from the pocket.

'What is it?' Andrew asked, obviously admiring the shiny medallion.

'It's a genuine Purple Heart,' Darin said in a low voice. 'It's like a very special military medal.'

Andrew's eyes glowed as he gently rubbed his finger over the engraved words. 'Where did you get it?' he asked.

Darin shoved the medal back into the secret pocket and zipped it shut. 'It's my dad's,' he said. 'He got it for being injured in the Gulf War.'

'Does he know you brought it?'

Darin shook his head, feeling a knot in his stomach. 'I'm going to put it back in his dresser drawer as soon as I get home today.'

'Your old man probably stole it.'

Darin turned to find Judd looking over his shoulder, grinning.

'What do you know, Judd?' Andrew said. 'Come on, Darin. We'd better hurry and get to our seats.'

The morning passed quickly and turned out to be a pretty good one for Darin, after all. He made an A on his history test and during the morning recess Judd vomited and was sent home by the school nurse.

All was well until after lunch, when Miss Poe announced that it was time for the oral reports. The students went to their lockers to get their things. That's when Darin discovered that the medal was missing!

***

'What do you think, Andrew?' Darin asked later when the boys were shooting baskets in P.E. 'Do you suppose Judd took the medal during recess when he went back to the classroom to get his things?'

Andrew nodded. 'He had to. No one else even knew it was in there.'

Darin slammed the basketball hard against the backboard, not even attempting a basket. 'What am I going to do, Andrew? I can't tell on him or my parents will find out for sure.'

'I don't know, Darin. I sure wouldn't want to be in your shoes right now!' Andrew exclaimed.

I Really Messed Up!

When he got home that afternoon, Darin grabbed a sandwich and started playing computer games, ignoring the chores list on the kitchen table.

'Darin,' Tamara called from the kitchen. 'Get in here and empty the trash.'

'Later,' he said. 'I'm busy right now.'

Tamara stomped into the den with the list in her hand. 'You'd better turn that thing off and get busy. Mom said to do your work before you played on the computer, and I want you to do my job of folding the towels from the dryer, too.'

'Yeah, right,' Darin muttered as he continued to play. 'In your dreams.'

'Fine with me,' Tamara said. 'I thought maybe you'd want to work out a deal so I won't tell Dad what I saw you stick in your backpack this morning.'

'Like I stuck something you would know about,' Darin said, his stomach starting to feel funny again.

'Like maybe a Purple Heart?' Tamara asked. 'You didn't even see me watching, did you?'

Darin looked up from his game. Tamara laughed. 'Looks like I have your attention now,' she said with a smirk.

'So what do you want?' Darin asked.

'Just do one chore for me each day and I will keep my mouth shut.' Tamara paused. 'Deal?'

'Like I have a choice?' Darin said. 'You said you want me to fold the towels?'

Tamara nodded. Darin closed his game and

hit the basement stairs. You'd better keep your word, Tamara, or I'll get even real bad.'

'Yeah, and you'd better get that thing back in Dad's drawer.'

'I know, I know.' Darin finished the chores and went up to his room. He definitely did not want to be around for small talk when his parents got home from work.

As Darin walked into his room, he noticed his Bible laying on the bookshelf next to his bed. The next day was Wednesday, and that evening he would attend the second meeting of the God Squad at church. Darin's youth pastor had chosen twelve guys and girls and was training them to be leaders among their peers at church and in their schools. Darin, the youngest member, was determined not to fall behind.

They would be discussing the Ten Commandments. Darin picked up his Bible and flopped across the bed. Opening to Exodus 20, he read through the list of commandments again, trying to concentrate on each one so he would have something to add to the discussion at the meeting.

Darin had grown up hearing the Ten Commandments and pretty much knew what they meant. But when he read the first six words of the fifth commandment, he froze. *Honor your father and your mother.* Beside the verse, in the margin of his Bible, was a definition for the word honor —to prize highly, to care for, to show respect for, to obey.

To obey. 'Man,' he said. 'Well, I've messed that one up already.'

At about 6:00, Darin's mother called him down for dinner. She had baked a frozen lasagne and made garlic bread to go along with it. This was one of Darin's favorite meals, but tonight he ate very little. Pushing his food around slowly, he hoped his mother wouldn't notice. But she did, and so did his father.

'Are you sick, Darin?' his father asked.

His mother looked alarmed and reached across the corner of the table to feel his forehead. 'You're not warm, honey. Is it your stomach?'

Tamara kicked Darin under the table. Darin glared at her. 'You'd better keep your mouth shut!' he said with his eyes.

'Darin?' Darin's mother was still waiting for an answer. What was the question? Darin panicked.

'Uh... I've just had a long day. I had a really hard history test, but I got an A.' Darin tried to perk up and did a good enough job to fool his parents. 'I guess I'll probably go to bed early tonight.'

'Which will mean that I won't have to stick around for family time. Perfect,' he thought.

Darin's father had suggested they study the Ten Commandments in their family devotions that week to reinforce what Darin was learning in his leadership group. Darin had liked the idea – hoping his parents would say something impressive he could claim for his own at the meeting.

'Darin,' his mother said. 'I talked to your teacher after school today when I stopped by to pay your basketball fees. She said you had a little trouble on the playground.'

His mother stopped there, her eyes open wide. Darin knew the look. She expected an explanation and it had better be good.

Darin's father cleared his throat and looked up from his plate. 'Well, son?'

Darin's goose was cooked and he knew it. He might as well spill his guts. He told his parents about the new boy at school and how, for some reason, he had decided to pick on Darin. He could tell that his parents were feeling really sorry for him. After all, Darin never caused trouble and they knew it. Of course, Darin didn't mention the missing medal.

'Well, I think you'd better steer clear of this young man,' Darin's mother suggested. 'Better to walk away from trouble.'

'That's true, dear,' Darin's father said. 'But I want Darin to defend himself. I don't want that kid beating up on him.'

'Wow! If looks could kill,' thought Darin, when he saw the look his mother shot his father. 'You go, Dad!' But even though Darin was cheering on the inside, he managed to keep a straight face on the outside. He wasn't totally stupid, you know.

'So you want me to fight back, Dad?' he asked, trying desperately not to grin.

'Absolutely not!' his mother practically shouted. 'I will not stand for your fighting at school!'

Darin looked at his father. 'Dad?' he dared whisper, being extremely careful not to look at his mother.

But his dad shook his head sadly. Well, it looked pretty sad to Darin. 'Your mother's right, son. I guess the kid in me just came out a little.' Then he sat up a bit straighter and added, 'But you let me know if that boy pushes you around again.'

Darin moaned.

'Is your homework finished, Darin?' his mother asked.

He nodded.

'Good. You can play on the computer for about ten minutes. Then we'll have our family devotions early so you can get to bed.'

'Sure, Mom,' Darin answered. He wasn't going to skip family time after all. Darin sighed then Tamara spoke up.

'Uh, Darin,' Tamara said. 'You promised to help with the dishes tonight, remember?'

Darin started to argue but took one look at his sister and changed his mind. He'd had enough trouble for one day. 'Oh, yeah. I remember,' he said.

* * *

When Tamara and Darin finished the dishes, they joined their parents in the family room for their nightly Bible study and prayer time. Darin usually loved this time, but this evening he dreaded it. His pretence at being tired hadn't worked - it would be family time

44

and then bed. Darin sighed. It had been worth a try.

'Let's see,' Darin's father said. 'We're in Exodus 20, aren't we, dear?'

'Yes,' Mrs Johnson said. 'We covered the first four of the Ten Commandments last night. We stopped after verse eleven.'

Darin's Bible fell open at the right place.

'Will you read the next commandment for us, Darin?' his father asked.

'Honor your father and your mother...' Darin swallowed, *'...so that you may live long in the land the Lord your God is giving you.'*

'My Sunday school teacher told us that this commandment is the first one God ever gave that has a promise attached to it,' Tamara said. 'We talked about when we don't really feel like honoring our parents — you know, like when we don't get our way or something.'

Darin fidgeted with the bookmark attached to his Bible, pinching his fingers around it and running them up and down the length of the ribbon.

'That's good, Tamara,' Mr Johnson said. 'Did you talk about how to go about honoring your parents?'

Tamara nodded. 'We should respect our parents in our speech and in our actions.'

Darin kept his eyes glued on his Bible.

'What about you, Darin,' his mother asked. 'In what other ways can we honor our parents?'

'With obedience?' he whispered. Darin thought about how his Dad told him not to take the medal to school but then he had taken it anyway. Darin looked over to his mother. 'Does that mean that if we disobey, we will die soon?'

Mrs Johnson glanced at her husband. He turned to Darin. 'Why do you ask that?' he said.

'Well, if we obey, God promises that we will live for a long time, so I was thinking that maybe the opposite is true if we disobey.'

Mr Johnson chuckled. 'I don't think so, son. You've been disobeying off and on for eleven years. That's what God's grace is all about.'

'God's grace?' Darin couldn't understand it. Tense and anxious he tried to work out his problems in his head. 'God will forgive me for disobeying my dad, but that still won't bring the medal back. Oh, God. What am I going to do?'

'Tamara, will you read the next verse?' Mr Johnson said.

'You shall not murder.'

Mrs Johnson smiled. 'I don't think we have to worry too much about this one, but it's still very important.'

'Well, there's another verse that sort of goes with this one, Mom,' Tamara said. 'We talked about it last Sunday, too.'

'Where's it found?' Mrs Johnson asked.

'Somewhere in 1 John. It says that anyone who hates his brother is a murderer. My teacher said that hate comes when we don't deal with anger and let it build up inside us.'

'That is so true,' Mr Johnson said. 'That's why God tells us not to let the sun go down on our anger.'

'Oh, God,' Darin prayed. 'This is getting worse. How do I stop being angry with Judd? What he did wasn't fair.'

'We have to make a decision to forgive even when we don't feel like it,' Darin's father continued.

'But how can you stop being angry when someone keeps picking on you?' Darin blurted out, his voice cracking in the middle.

Can I Get Out Of This Alive?

The next morning, Judd walked up as Darin was putting away his jacket and backpack. 'Hey, Darin,' he said, pulling him aside. 'My mom said I better apologize to you for the other day. My little brother was out there and saw what I did to you. Anyway, if I don't make friends with you, my mom's going to tell my dad.' Judd had Darin cornered.

Other students were looking in their direction to see what was going on. Darin recognized the chance to prove that he was a

Christian by forgiving Judd in front of his friends. But it just didn't seem fair. Judd had taken his father's medal. He didn't deserve forgiveness.

'So, what do you say?' Judd asked.

Darin pushed past Judd. 'Whatever,' he said. Darin felt sick inside. He knew he was doing exactly the opposite of what God wanted him to do, and as he started to walk away, Hannah caught his eye and smiled sadly. Darin knew she had overheard. The verse Tamara had talked about the night before came to his mind. *Anyone who hates his brother is a murderer.* 'Help me do this for you, God,' he prayed silently, turning around again to face Judd who was following him.

'Listen, Judd. I forgive you for picking on me.'

Judd took a step back — his eyebrows arched. 'You do?'

Darin nodded, whispering another silent prayer. 'Help me to really mean this, God.'

Then Judd said something else, 'My mom told me all about that Purple Heart. Did your dad get shot or something?'

Darin stared at Judd in disbelief. Does he really think I don't know he took it? Darin wondered.

'What's he talking about, Darin?' his friend, Brett, asked him. 'What medal?'

'Great,' Darin thought. 'Now what do I say? If the whole class hears about this medal going missing then my parents will find out for sure!'

Fortunately, Andrew happened to walk up just at that time. 'Hey, Brett,' he said. 'Darin was going to do his oral report on the medal yesterday but he changed his mind about showing the thing. Sort of gives him the creeps to talk about it. You know what I mean?'

Brett nodded and went to his seat. The other students followed him to their seats. The morning sped by and before Darin realized it, it was time for recess.

Darin raised his hand. 'Miss Poe, could I

please stay in a few minutes to finish my maths homework? I have basketball practice after school and I have a lot of other homework. We have that science test tomorrow, you know.'

Miss Poe smiled. 'Yes, Darin. You may finish your work. But don't stay in the whole recess. You need some fresh air.'

Darin nodded and busily spread his maths book and homework page out on his desk. With his head down, he pretended to be deep in concentration as the other students followed Miss Poe from the room. He gave himself a few minutes, just to be sure no one returned to the room, then dashed to the closet to inspect Judd's backpack. Darin had heard that Judd's father helped build highways and moved his family around in a travel trailer every couple of months. There wouldn't be many places to hide a medal in a travel trailer, Darin figured. Judd must have the medal with him.

It wasn't hard to find Judd's bag. Instead

of a cloth bag with shoulder pads and straps, Judd carried a plastic grocery bag. Digging inside, Darin found only a bread-and-butter pickle, a half a bag of chips, and a hard-boiled egg. Darin felt sorry for Judd again. He shook the bag. Maybe Judd didn't take the medal after all. But who else could have?

Disappointed, Darin hung the bag back on the hook. But, running his hand down the side to push it back in with the other bags, he felt something hard down in the corner. Yes! It was hard, flat, and round. Darin shot his hand down in the bag again and dug for the medal.

It was wrapped round and round in a wrinkled handkerchief. Beads of sweat formed on Darin's forehead. He was relieved, but also angry. He knew that he could never tell on Judd — the bully would just get away with everything. All Darin could do was stick the medal deep in his pocket, take it home, and put it back in his dad's dresser drawer.

Quickly, he unwrapped the handkerchief to

get the... What? Two quarters! Fifty cents? Darin was sick. 'I ought to keep this so he'll realize how it feels to have something stolen from him.' Where was the medal? Darin shoved the money back in the bag and ran to Judd's desk. Frantically, he rummaged through the books and unzipped Judd's pencil bag.

'Darin?' It was Miss Poe. 'What are you doing in Judd's desk? I thought you wanted to work on your maths.'

Darin looked up. 'M-M-Miss Poe,' he stuttered. 'Why did you come back inside?' Darin was in shock, but even in shock, he knew he had asked a really dumb question.

Miss Poe marched over to Judd's desk and shut the lid. 'Young man,' she said. 'I think it's time we had a talk with your parents, don't you?'

Darin looked up, but his mouth wouldn't work. His eyes wouldn't blink. His heart? Yes, his heart was beating. So hard that he thought it was going to pop right out of his chest. Miss

Poe was still staring at him, and Darin couldn't think of a single thing to say.

It just didn't seem fair. Sure, he had taken the medal without asking. But how did he know some bully cousin of Mr Trelunki's would enrol in school that day? The medal would have been fine if it weren't for Judd. Darin sighed. 'It's hopeless. I am not going to get out of this alive.'

Then he had an idea.

Okay, I'll Talk!

Alone in his bedroom, Darin looked at the sealed envelope in his hands. What had Miss Poe written? Darin tried to figure out what to do. He could forget to give his parents the note. No. That would never work.

'Do not be overcome by evil, but overcome evil with good.'

Darin had read the verse from Romans 12 in his devotions just that morning. Well, he thought, he really didn't have much of a choice. He would have to tell the truth, the whole

truth, and nothing but the truth. But first...
he had a lot to do.

Darin shoved the envelope under his pillow
and ran downstairs. Grabbing his jacket and
some supplies, he headed out to the garage to
get the ladder. Darin's mom had been bugging
his dad for weeks to clean the kitchen
windows. One time she even threatened to
drop kick him out the door if he didn't get
busy. Darin and his Dad had laughed, but
judging by the look on her face, his mom had
definitely not thought it was funny.

Anyway, now the job would get done, and his
mom would be in a great mood. Then he would
confess – before he gave his mom the note.
Yes. Mom would read it and understand. Then
she could explain it to Dad and maybe he
wouldn't get so mad. Darin shook himself. There
was no time to be worrying about how all that
would turn out now. He had a lot to do.

After the windows were sparkling clean,
Darin picked up all the rotten apples that had

fallen to the ground under the apple tree. Yuk! Some were so squishy they leaked mush and juice all over his hands. Oh, well. He had a plan and the plan had to be carried out carefully.

Just as he finished dumping the rotten apples on the compost pile and was putting the ladder back in the garage, Darin's parents pulled into the driveway from work. 'Perfect!' he thought.

Sure enough, they wanted to know what he had been doing with the ladder. Darin told them and waited for their praise. But they said nothing. They just looked at each other and nodded. Scary. What was going on?

'Don't you like your surprise, Mom? You wanted those windows washed, didn't you?'

'Yes, Darin,' she answered. 'Let's go inside now. I need to start supper.'

Darin turned around to talk to his dad, but he had already gone into the house through the garage. 'Something wrong, Mom?' he asked.

There went her eyebrows again. 'You tell me, Darin,' was all she said. Then she followed Dad into the house.

Later, at the supper table, Darin's parents ate quietly. Darin could feel the tension. 'Wow!' he thought. 'They must have had some humdinger of a fight on the way home.'

Darin and his sister said very little. They weren't totally ignorant. They knew when to keep their mouths shut. Anyway, supper was almost over before anyone said a word.

'Children,' Mom began.

'Oh, great!' Darin thought. 'She never calls us that unless we are in major trouble. Did she talk to Miss Poe? No, that couldn't be it. She wouldn't have included Tamara.'

Suddenly, Darin saw something funny. Tamara, who had really been taking advantage of Darin the last few days, almost choked on her peas. She totally did not expect for her mother to yell at her for anything. Darin loved the fear he saw in Tamara's eyes.

'Ha!' he thought. 'Serves you right.'

But then he felt it. The stare. Both Mom and Dad were looking at him, and believe me, they were not smiling. That was when Darin realized he was actually grinning. He immediately wiped that smile from his face. 'Yes, Mother?' he said, with as much politeness as he could muster.

Darin's mother took a deep breath and exhaled slowly, blowing the air out her nose. Darin saw her look at his father, and he nodded. 'Go ahead, dear,' he said.

'Oh, double-great!' Darin thought. 'They're not mad at each other. That can only mean one thing — they're mad at us!' Suddenly, Darin's stomach began to roll. Could he get away with being sick? No. That would make them madder. He'd better sit up straight and take it like a man. Whatever it was.

'Go ahead, Mom,' he said. Tamara kicked him under the table.

Darin's mother smiled. Well, just a little.

Then she released the bullet. 'This morning, when I was putting away some laundry, I noticed that your father's Purple Heart was missing from the dresser drawer,' she said.

Tamara gasped. 'Your Purple Heart?' she whispered, looking at her father. 'The one they gave you from the Gulf War?'

'Good one, Tamara,' Darin thought, with disgust. 'You actually fooled me with that shocked look.' Then Darin realized that he, too, must play this game. Tamara was going to be a hard act to follow!

'Are you sure, Mom?' he asked. 'Maybe it just slipped to the bottom of the drawer or something.'

'No, Darin,' his mother answered flatly. 'It is gone.'

Mashed potatoes that Darin had just swallowed came sliding back up into his throat, and he started to heave. Swallowing the potatoes a second time, he scrambled to get control. He had to think about what to do next.

The truth, the whole truth, and nothing but the truth. That was the only way.

'I don't know anything about it,' Darin said, trying to sound as innocent as possible.

'Me, either,' Tamara said. 'Maybe we can help you look for it.'

'No!' Darin's father shouted. 'Maybe you'd better tell me where it is, and maybe you'd better tell me right now!'

Darin gulped. His father stood, his fist coming down hard on the table. By now there were little veins bulging from his neck and his ears were flaming red.

'Dear...' Darin's mother said quietly.

'Dear, nothing!' he said. 'These kids know what happened and they'll stay in their rooms the rest of their lives if they don't own up!'

Tamara kicked Darin again. Hard. Crunch time. This wasn't going to get any better.

'Okay,' Darin said, holding the sides of his chair so tightly his knuckles turned white. 'I'll talk.'

Please Dad!
Don't Do That!

Everything happened at once. It was like slow motion. Darin's mother started crying, Tamara spilled her milk, and the phone rang. Darin watched as the others grabbed napkins and raced to stop the river of milk before it ran off onto the carpet. It was a nightmare, and it ended just as the phone stopped ringing and the answering machine kicked in. Tamara and her parents sunk down into their chairs — exhausted. A pile of drenched napkins lay wadded on the garlic bread platter. No one moved. Everyone heard it. First the beep. Then... 'Mr and Mrs Johnson, this is Miss Poe, Darin's teacher. I told you I would call if there were any further problems at school with your son. I just wanted to be sure you received the note I sent home with him today, and I wondered if you had any questions. Please feel free to call me this evening if you do.' Click.

Darin burst into tears. It was too much. His head was splitting from trying to figure out what to do next. He couldn't take it any more.

'Where is the note, Darin?' his mother asked.

'It's u-u-under my p-pillow,' he stammered. 'I'll g-get it.'

'You stay seated,' his father said. 'Tamara, go get the note.'

Darin accepted a handkerchief from his father and dried his eyes. He took a drink of his milk to stop his hiccups. Tamara returned with the envelope and handed it to her father.

'We are going into the study, Tamara,' he

said. 'I want you to clean off this table and do the dishes. If we need you, we will come and get you. Do you understand?'

Tamara nodded and began stacking the dinner plates.

Darin followed his parents into the study and sat down on the sofa next to his mother. His father shut the door and pulled up a chair in front of Darin.

'Now, son,' he said. 'Tell us what is going on.'

It didn't take long for Darin to tell the facts, and this time, he didn't leave anything out. Somewhere in the middle of the story, his mother scooted close and put her arm around him. When he finished, he waited. He knew his father was trying to think of something really wise to say. He also knew a consequence coming — a big one.

After what seemed like eternity, his father spoke. 'Well, son, I'm glad you've finally decided to tell the truth. I'm sure it's a relief to you, too."

Darin nodded.

'You knew it was wrong to take the medal, didn't you?'

'Yes, sir,' Darin said.

'And you also knew better than to lie to us about it.'

'Yes, sir.'

'And because you lied, you couldn't come to us for help with this Judd Becker kid.'

Darin nodded. Mr Johnson folded his hands and looked at Darin with sadness in his eyes for several seconds. Darin knew he was in serious trouble, but could feel the love in his father's expression. Tears poured now as Darin realized how much he had disappointed his father. 'I wish he would just get angry. That would be easier than this.'

'We've talked about the Ten Commandments the last few nights, Darin, and I know you are aware that you have broken several of them.'

Darin nodded, looking at his trembling hands.

'Look me in the eye, son,' his father said. Darin lifted his chin. 'Now I want to tell you about someone in the Bible who also broke those commandments. It's in the book of Romans. You remember Paul, don't you?'

'Yes.'

'He struggled with the same spiritual problem you and I struggle with.'

'You struggle?' Darin asked — his eyes wide with surprise.

Mr Johnson patted Darin's shoulder and his mother reached over and hugged him. 'Of course I do, Darin,' his father said. 'We all do. In fact, I want to ask your forgiveness right now for getting so angry at the table.'

'But you had a right to be angry, Dad.'

'I may have had a right, but the Bible says to be angry and sin not. I sinned when I yelled and lost control. I was especially angry because I knew you had deliberately disobeyed me.'

Darin gulped. 'You knew?'

'We knew as soon as we got home and found

you doing chores without being asked,' Darin's mother said. 'What was that all about?'

Darin hung his head. 'I read in my devotions this morning that we should overcome evil with good.' Darin saw his father start to grin and then cough to cover it up. 'What's so funny?' he thought.

'The Bible says to overcome evil, Darin, not cover it up. Did you think doing good would undo the mistakes you had made?'

'Not really,' Darin said. 'I just thought it might put you in a better mood before I gave you the note from Miss Poe.'

Darin's father coughed again. 'Let's get back to Paul. I think there's a lesson for you, son.'

'It's in Romans 7,' Darin's mother said, opening her Bible. 'Listen to what Paul said. "*I do not understand what I do. For what I want to do I do not do, but what I hate I do.*"'

'It says that?' Darin asked.

Mrs Johnson smiled. 'Life is all about becoming more like Jesus, Darin. That's why

His mercy and grace are so precious.'

'God doesn't expect us to be perfect, but he does expect us to be honest with him and with each other,' Darin's father said. 'We need to get ready for church now.'

Darin groaned. He'd forgotten all about the God squad and the Ten Commandments lessons. What a mess! Darin's father ignored him and continued, 'I'm not sure what we're going to do about this, but I do know that we are going to get to the bottom of it. Then we'll decide what sort of consequence is appropriate. What do you think?'

Darin's mother nodded. 'I think I need to call Miss Poe back to let her know what's going on and to see if she has Judd Becker's phone number. We definitely need to speak with his parents, and the sooner the better.'

'No!' Darin cried. 'Please, Dad! Don't do that. Please!'

'Darin, we don't have any choice,' his father said. 'That medal is important to me and I want it back. Besides, that boy has something that doesn't belong to him.'

'Please, Dad,' Darin continued. 'I'll ask him for it tomorrow. I promise.'

Darin's father shook his head. 'I'm sorry, son, but this is the way it has to be. Now I want you to go upstairs and get ready.'

'Mom?' Darin looked at his mother, his eyes begging her to help him.

'Get going, Darin,' was all she said.

Get Your Fat Finger Out Of His Face!

The next morning Darin was called to the office right after the pledges. When he got there, he saw Judd sitting on a chair beside his father. They were not smiling. Darin tried to ignore them as he walked to the counter.

Mr Trelunki told Darin to take a seat in his office, and asked Judd and his parents to join them. Darin gulped when he walked into the office and saw his parents already seated by the wall. They smiled slightly and pointed to a chair between them. Darin sat down.

The Becker family sat across from Darin's family. Mr Trelunki sat at his desk.

'Well, folks,' Mr Trelunki began. 'I guess you all know why we're here.' Then he stared back and forth between Darin and Judd.

'Yes, sir,' the boys said at the same time.

'Darin,' Mr Trelunki said, his glasses slipping down his nose. 'Judd's parents were very shocked when your parents telephoned last night and said you had accused Judd of taking your father's medal.'

Darin felt his ears burning.

'What do you have to say, young man?'

Darin tried to speak, but his tongue felt like it was too big for his mouth.

'Ralph, I think we all know the story,' Mr Becker said. 'What I want to know is why this kid would make up such a lie about our little Judd.' Mr Becker put his arm around his son and squeezed his shoulder.

Darin couldn't be sure that it really was a friendly squeeze. It seemed more like a mad squeeze, even though the man had a smile on his face. Judd winced.

Darin's father cleared his throat and everyone looked in his direction. He turned to face Judd's father. 'My son did wrong by taking my medal without asking. There is no denying that, and I will deal with him later. But from the get-go, Mr Becker, your son has been picking on my son, and that needs to stop.'

Mr Becker stood to talk, but when he opened his mouth, a meaty belch escaped. 'Excuse me,' he said. 'But I want you to know that I tanned this boy's hide for picking a fight with your son the first day of school, and he ain't done it since.' Mr Becker grabbed Judd's arm and yanked him to his feet. Sticking his finger in Judd's face, Mr Becker asked, 'What I'm saying's the truth, ain't it boy?'

Judd turned white. 'Y-yes, sir,' he answered. Mr Becker pushed Judd back down on his chair. Then he walked over to Darin and stuck a finger in his face.

'Darin,' he said. 'You're telling me that Judd took that medal. You really believe that, son?'

Darin nodded, sliding back in his chair.

Mr Becker continued. 'I'm going to find out, son, and believe me, Judd will be sorry if I find out he's lying.' Mr Becker looked at Judd, shook his finger, and turned back to Darin. 'But if I find out you're lying, kid, you are going to have to answer for your story. Understand?'

'Just one minute!' Darin's father jumped up and yelled in Mr Becker's face. 'You get your fat finger out of my son's face!'

Mr Becker drew his arm back and made a fist. 'Why, you...'

Somewhere in there, Mr Trelunki jumped over his desk and grabbed Mr Becker's arm. 'Hold on there, fellows,' he said. 'This is no way to settle this. Please take your seats, both of you.'

'You go, Dad!' Darin thought. The two fathers sat down. Darin could hear their heavy breathing and watched their shoulders move up and down, almost in rhythm. Darin looked at Judd. Forgetting the trouble they were in for a minute, the two boys couldn't help but grin. This was getting pretty good.

Mr Trelunki decided to call an end to the meeting and promised to get to the bottom of this mystery. Darin thought the worst was over until Mr Trelunki announced that Darin and Judd would serve detention every day after school until the truth came out.

'That's not fair,' Judd blurted out. 'I didn't do anything.'

Darin almost believed him. But there was no other answer. Judd had to have the medal.

As the boys returned to class, they walked down opposite sides of the hall. Just before entering the classroom, however, Judd grabbed Darin's shirt tail and muttered, 'You're dead meat!'

Apologize To Judd!

The day wasn't over before Darin and Judd were back in the office — this time for fighting. Mr Trelunki suspended them both for one day and called their fathers to come and get them. Darin's father had arrived first and was now behind the closed door with Mr Trelunki.

He'd only been there for a few minutes when Mr Becker walked into the office, his clothes covered with tar, his hair a greasy mess. He stared at Judd long and hard with narrowed eyes, slowly shaking his head back and forth.

Judd flinched when his father reached over to grab his hat and threw it on the floor. 'What's this doing on your head in the building, boy?' he bellowed. Never mind that Mr Becker's hat was still on his head.

'I'm s-sorry, sir,' Judd mumbled. 'I guess I wasn't thinking.'

'Well, I guess you'd better start thinking, mister!' his father said. Then he snapped his fingers and pointed his shaking index finger in Darin's direction. 'You'd better be thinking too, boy,' he said.

'Excuse, me. Mr Becker. May I help you?' It was the school secretary. 'I need to check my son out of school,' Mr Becker said. 'Just show me where to sign and we'll be going.'

Darin looked at Judd and noticed tears in his eyes. He felt sorry for Judd. It wasn't too hard to figure out where Judd got his temper and foul mouth.

'Mr Trelunki would like to have a word with you before you leave,' the secretary said. She turned to her desk and pushed the intercom button. Shortly, Mr Trelunki and Mr Johnson stepped into the outer office. Mr Trelunki extended his hand and Mr Becker shook it.

'Sorry to call you off the job,' Mr Trelunki said. 'But fighting at school is not tolerated and these boys need to know that.'

All three adults turned and stared at the boys. Darin's stomach hurt. He had to go to the bathroom, but was afraid to ask. Then something happened that made him forget all about needing to go the bathroom.

Hannah walked into the office and handed Mr Trelunki a note. Darin was embarrassed. But Hannah smiled. Darin could read compassion in her eyes.

Mr Trelunki read the note and handed it to Darin's father. He read it and handed it to Mr Becker. Then Mr Becker snorted and said, 'I told you so.'

Darin got a funny feeling in his stomach. Actually, it wasn't funny at all. He could tell the letter said something that was going to change everything. And he sensed that it wasn't going to be in his favor because the men were now glaring at him.

Out of the corner of his eye, Darin caught a tiny smile on Judd's face. Darin's blood boiled inside him. He could feel the sweat pop out on his forehead, but he didn't dare move to wipe it off. He squeezed his legs together tightly. Now he really had to go.

Mr Trelunki thanked Hannah and sent her back to class. Then he turned and gave the boys one of those 'I've had enough of this!' looks. 'Boys,' he said, 'Come into my office.'

Judd looked at Darin and Darin looked at Judd.

'Now!' Mr Trelunki roared.

That's all it took. Darin jumped up and followed Judd into the office. As it turned out, the letter explained that on the day the medal disappeared, Hannah had returned to the classroom for a jump rope and was there when Judd came back from the nurse's office for his backpack. Judd had not gone near Darin's backpack or anyone else's, for that matter. Judd could not have taken the medal.

Darin couldn't believe what he was hearing. If not Judd, who took the medal? Hannah? He knew she would never do such a thing. Besides, she didn't even know it was in there.

'Darin!' It was his father. 'Did you hear me?' Darin shook his head. 'I said to apologize to Judd and his father at once for all the trouble you have caused.'

Darin's ears began to burn when he glanced over and saw a cocky look on Judd's face, but he knew he had no choice but to respond. 'I'm sorry for my mistake, Judd, and I'm sorry you had to take time off work to come down to school, Mr Becker.'

'Twice,' Mr Becker said, his eyebrows raised.

Darin nodded. 'I'm very sorry,' he said.

'And I want to apologize for my behavior this morning, too,' Darin's father said to Mr Becker.

'Aw, don't worry about it. I've been known to lose my cool once in a while, too.'

Darin almost laughed. He looked at his dad. Now his ears were turning red.

'Well, I guess boys will be boys,' Mr Becker said, slapping Mr Trelunki on the back. 'I'm just glad it's you, not me, that has to deal with them every day, Ralphie — er, Mr Trelunki.'

Judd was still suspended for beating Darin up at recess, but it didn't look like he was going to be in too much trouble. Mr Becker actually looked proud of his son when Mr Trelunki mentioned the fight. 'I guess Darin got what was coming to him,' Mr Becker said as he was leaving. 'Maybe now, he'll try harder to get along with my boy.'

When Darin got home, his father sent him to his room to think about what he had done.

'After you clean up, I want you to think about what consequence is appropriate, son,' he told Darin. 'Then your mother and I will discuss it with you after supper.'

Darin sat on his bed. Waiting was the worst. A few hours later, he heard his mother pull in the driveway. He went to the window and watched his father walk out to the car to help carry in groceries. The knot in his stomach tightened.

Stretching out on his bed, Darin pulled his pillow from under the covers. Hugging it to himself, he began to cry. This whole situation just kept getting more complicated. Darin almost looked forward to his punishment so his parents wouldn't be angry and life could return to normal. But then he remembered something. The medal was still missing. His father's purple heart was gone.

After a while, Darin's mother knocked on the door and came into his room. Darin squeezed his eyes shut and tried to lie perfectly still. Mrs Johnson sat on the edge of the bed and rubbed Darin's back.

'Want to tell me about it, honey?' Darin didn't move. 'I love you, Darin, and I want to help you. I know you need someone to talk to.'

His mother's love got to him, and Darin opened his eyes and sat up. Leaning on his mother's shoulder he began to cry. She held him as he tried to tell her the story between sobs.

'Judd started the fight. I tried to forgive him, but he wouldn't quit picking on me. Then, when some of the guys in the class found out Judd didn't take the medal, they blamed me for getting Judd in trouble. They just wanted to get on Judd's good side.' Darin sat up and wiped his eyes. 'I didn't even fight back, Mom. I don't know why I got in trouble.'

Mrs Johnson wiped Darin's hair out of his face. 'Let's think about what you just said, Darin. I'm glad you didn't start the fight, but you have done plenty to get yourself in trouble, haven't you?'

'Yes, but...'

'Stop there, son. You need to take responsibility for your own actions — regardless of what Judd did to provoke you.'

'How do I do that?' Darin asked.

'You get down on your knees and admit your sin to God and ask his forgiveness. He will wipe away the sin and the guilt that is probably making you sick right now.'

Fresh tears poured down Darin's cheeks. 'How did you know?' he asked.

'I've sinned, too, Darin. I know what it's like to disappoint God.'

Darin climbed off his bed and knelt beside it. 'Will you help me pray, Mom?'

'I'll pray with you, but you need to do this on your own. It is between you and God. Just talk to him like you're talking to me.'

Darin shut his eyes. 'Dear God,' he began. 'I'm so sorry for this mess. I'm sorry for breaking your Ten Commandments. For not honoring my parents by respecting and obeying them. For stealing my dad's medal from his drawer. For telling the other kids that Judd stole the medal when I didn't really know that for sure.'

Darin looked up. His mother had her head bowed in prayer. She wasn't finished. Darin shut his eyes again and continued. 'Please forgive me for hating Judd, and please help us find Dad's medal.'

We All Make Mistakes

Darin woke up early the next morning. He pulled on his jeans and a sweatshirt. Then he remembered. He was suspended from school.

He could hear his parents in the kitchen as he walked down the stairs and wondered if they would mention the deal with the medal. Supper had come and gone the night before, and they'd both acted like nothing at all had happened. Darin had even tried to bring the matter up, but his mother had changed the subject.

Darin walked into the kitchen and sat down. His mother set a cereal bowl and a glass of juice in front of him like always. His father put on his jacket and poured a cup of coffee to take with him on his drive to work.

Passing Darin on his way out the door, he playfully ruffled his hair. 'Glad you're up early, Darin,' he said. 'Mom has quite a list of chores for you to do today. You'll have to work pretty steady to get it all done before we come home this evening.'

Darin looked up. 'But what if I...'

Mr Johnson smiled. You know — one of those 'I don't even want to talk about it' smiles. 'No what if, son. I expect every bit of it done and done right. Understand?'

'Yes, sir.'

As soon as his family was gone, Darin tackled the list of jobs. After he swept the patio and cleaned the bathrooms, he began to dust his mother's knick-knacks. He had just about finished when he slipped on a rug and dropped a porcelain vase. Water ran across the hardwood floor and flowers flew in every direction.

'Oh, great!' Darin said. 'Now I'm really in trouble.' He cleaned up the mess and finished the dusting. Then he stuck his dust cloth on the end of a broom and cleaned cobwebs out of every corner of the house. He wet a cleaning rag and washed the top of the water heater and scrubbed soap scum from around the rim of the washing machine.

When he stopped for lunch, he was exhausted, and only halfway through the list. Mrs Johnson had left a sack lunch on the counter for him and as Darin pulled out a sandwich, chips, and a banana, he noticed a note in the bottom of the bag. It was from his parents.

Darin, We love you and forgive you for the things you have done. We all make mistakes, son. It's not the end of the world. You are still the best son a parent could ever ask for, and we are still very proud of you. Be willing to learn from your mistakes, Darin, and God will use them to help you grow to be more like him. We'll see you tonight.

Love, Mom and Dad

You Had It?
How Did You Get It?

Darin ate the last of his vegetables and finished his milk. For as long as he could remember, his mother had served broccoli when she fried chicken strips. Darin despised broccoli. But tonight, she had served corn. Darin glanced over at his mother and smiled.

Dinner was almost over. Darin had worked hard on his chores, but was still nowhere near finished by the time Tamara came home from school. When she saw the list, she offered to help, and together, they finished just as their parents came home from work. His mother had approved of the work and had praised Darin and Tamara for working together. Darin was still a bit suspicious as to why Tamara had been so quick to offer her help. It wasn't like her to care if he got in trouble.

Darin dreaded the lecture that he knew was coming. His father said very little during dinner, except to congratulate Tamara on winning the school spelling bee. Tamara was very proud about passing that test. After dinner, Darin's father asked Tamara to show them her ribbon. She went to get her backpack and brought it to the dining room table. As she shuffled through an assortment of papers, folders, and candy wrappers, Darin noticed a funny look on his father's face.

'Tamara,' he said. 'May I please see your school bag?'

She pulled out the award ribbon and quickly snapped the bag shut. 'Here's the ribbon, Daddy. I found it.'

Darin's father nodded and commented on her ribbon. Then he asked Tamara again to hand him the backpack.

'Daddy,' she said. 'I've got private letters and things in there. Please don't.'

But Mr Johnson kept his hand out and Tamara reluctantly handed him the bag. He reached in and pulled out a shiny object — the Purple Heart.

Their mother gasped. Darin practically choked on his dessert. Tamara started to cry.

'Y-you had it?' Darin asked. 'How did you get it?'

Mr Johnson repeated the question. 'How did you get this, Tamara?'

In between tears and sobs, Tamara told her story. She had seen Darin take the medal from his father's underwear drawer before school and decided she should teach him a lesson. When she knew his class would be gone for art, she asked for a hall pass. Supposedly, she needed to give her brother some lunch money.

Then she simply walked into his empty classroom and took the medal from his bag.

Darin's ears burned when he thought about all the chores he had done for Tamara to keep her quiet. And all along, she knew exactly where the medal was.

'I was going to put it back in your drawer, Daddy,' she cried. 'Honest.'

'Then why didn't you?' he asked.

'I overheard Darin talking to Andrew on the phone that night about how he was sure Judd Becker took it. I felt sorry for Darin because Judd had been bullying him at school and on the bus. I wanted Judd to get in trouble, so I just let everyone think he took it.' This time Tamara started crying so hard she got the hiccups. 'I didn't know everyone was going to make such a big deal out of everything. I was going to sneak it back in the drawer in a week or so.'

Mrs Johnson reached over and took Tamara's hand. 'Dear,' she said, 'your intentions may have seemed good at the time, but dishonesty is never the right choice.'

'I know,' Tamara sobbed, squeezing her mother's fingers.

'Darin,' Mr Johnson said. 'I've always told you not to be afraid to come to us with a problem. I understand why you thought Judd took the medal. I might have made the same mistake myself.'

Darin looked at his father. Was he softening? Darin couldn't believe his luck. But just as he was about to breathe a sigh of relief, he was cut short.

'What does upset me, though,' his father continued, 'is your dishonesty Darin and Tamara's and the lack of respect you showed in taking my medal without asking.'

'I'm sorry, Dad.'

Mr Johnson nodded. 'I'm sure you are, son.' He turned to look at Tamara who had stopped crying by this time. 'I'm sure you are both sorry.'

Darin's parents talked a little longer about the difference between being sorry you're caught and sorry about something you've done. Then they grounded Darin and Tamara for a month. This included the church youth tour the following weekend, they explained.

Tamara tried to argue that it wasn't Christian to take away a ministry trip as a punishment, but all that got her was another fifteen minute lecture on how long it takes to earn back trust.

Mrs Johnson suggested she clean the table and load the dishwasher later so the family could meet right then for their family devotions. 'I think we need to spend some time reading Gods' word and praying to him.'

'Good idea,' Mr Johnson said.

Darin and Tamara went upstairs to get their Bibles and joined their parents in the family room. Tamara plopped down next to her mother on the sofa. Mr Johnson was sitting in his recliner to the right of the sofa, and Darin settled into a rocking chair on the other side.

'I'd like to turn back to Exodus 20 one more time,' Darin's father said. 'I know we've covered the Ten Commandments, but I want to make one more point tonight.'

'Oh, great,' Darin thought. 'Let's just rub it in a little more, Dad.' Immediately, though, Darin felt ashamed of his attitude. His dad was actually being pretty cool about all this.

'I want to read through these commands and discuss how each one applies to this situation. Then, after we pray, we are going to put the matter behind us, once and for all.'

'You mean you want to forget that I almost lost your Purple Heart?' Darin asked.

'Yes,' his father answered. 'And I will tell you why in a few minutes.'

'Wow!' Darin thought. 'My dad is the most awesome, forgiving Christian I know.'

'I would like for you to read the first commandment, Darin.'

'You shall have no other gods before me.'

'What do you think became a god to you in this situation?'

Darin swallowed. A god? Then he realized the point his father was trying to make. 'I guess the Purple Heart. I thought it would make the other kids think I was really cool. That sounded so good that I was even willing to disobey you.'

'That's how the devil works, Darin,' his mother said. 'He tricks us by making something evil look really good.'

'Dad's Purple Heart is evil?' Tamara blurted out. 'What's up with that?'

Mrs Johnson smiled. 'It's not the medal, itself. It was the idea that a medal could bring honor and respect to Darin.'

'You kids — well, your mom and I, too — need to remember that. Satan will use a lot of things to tempt us. We must remember that if something causes us to go against what we know is right, it is not a good thing.'

Darin sort of understood. 'Like taking the

medal to school made me break God's commandment to honor my father and mother and not to steal.' His parents nodded. 'And then I blamed Judd for stealing it. That's kind of like giving false testimony against someone, isn't it, Dad?'

'Yes.'

'And hating Judd was like murder according to the Bible, wasn't it?' Darin felt sick at his stomach. Hot tears escaped from his eyes and rolled down his cheeks. His father walked over and knelt in front of Darin's chair. He pulled his son to his shoulder and held him in his arms.

'God will forgive you, Darin, and so will I.'

'But I d-d-don't deserve to be f-forgiven,' Darin whimpered. 'How could I be so bad when I try to be so good?'

'Remember Paul?' Mrs Johnson asked. 'He was a great man of God, but he had the same question.'

Darin pulled away from his father and nodded. He wiped his eyes with a tissue that

Tamara had gone and gotten. Looking his father directly in the eyes, he said, 'I'm really sorry, Dad.'

Mr Johnson reached for Darin's hand. 'I know, son, and I do forgive you and Tamara,' he said pointedly looking at his daughter's blushing face. 'The point I wanted to make tonight is that when God forgives our sins, he throws them into the sea of forgetfulness. We can't actually forget when we forgive, but we can make a decision not to bring it up again or think about it.'

'Never?' Darin asked.

'Never. If God can let it go, so can we. Now, I think it's time to pray.'

Darin's family knelt together by the sofa. Darin and Tamara prayed for forgiveness for what they had done. Then their parents each prayed a blessing over them and thanked God for their children and for what they had all learned over the last few days.

By the time they finished, Darin's stomach

no longer felt sick. Instead, he felt a warm love from his family and knew that God forgave him and still loved him.

'I think I'm ready for some ice cream,' Mr Johnson said, standing. 'Anybody want to join me?'

'Mom?' Darin said. 'I'd like to do the dishes for the family. Sort of my way of saying I'm really sorry.'

'I think that would be nice.'

After eating three bowls of ice cream, Darin cleared the table and loaded the dishwasher. Heading up to his room, he passed the family room.

'Darin,' his mother called. 'I just talked to Miss Poe on the phone. I told her you would want to make a public apology in front of the class, and she said you could do it first thing Monday morning.'

There's Something Else I Need To Say

Darin's father dropped him off at school Monday morning so he wouldn't have to face Judd on the bus.

'Bye, Dad,' Darin said as he pushed the car door shut. Darin went to the office to sign back in after his day of suspension. As he wrote his name on the chart, Mr Trelunki entered the room.

'Good morning, Darin,' he said. 'Got a minute?'

Darin nodded... and thought to himself.

'Got a minute he asks? He's the principal. If he says the word I've got all day.'

Mr Trelunki opened his office door and motioned for Darin to come in and sit down.

'I explained to your class what happened, Darin, and I'd like us all to put it behind us. But first, let's talk about Judd.' He paused — thinking carefully about what to say next. 'He's different than most of your friends. He can be tough to get along with, can't he?'

Darin had to think fast. If he said yes, he'd be insulting one of the principal's family. But if he said no, he'd be disagreeing with the principal and, worse yet, lying. 'Judd's pretty hard to get to know, I guess.'

Mr Trelunki chuckled. 'I know he can be a bully. I talked to your friend Andrew on Friday. He told me all about how Judd has treated you since his first day of school.'

Darin's eyes widened. He worked his fingers together, one over the other; his toes curled under tightly in his shoes.

Mr Trelunki walked over to Darin and patted his shoulder. 'Relax, Darin. You're not in more trouble. I just want you to know I'm on top of things. I've spoken to Miss Poe, and we're going to put a stop to Judd's misbehavior.'

Darin nodded again, afraid he'd cry if he tried to speak.

'I want you to promise to come to me if you have any more problems with Judd, okay?'

'Yes, sir,' Darin answered, fighting back tears. Why was Mr Trelunki being so nice? 'Mr Trelunki. There's something else I need to say.'

'Go ahead, son.'

'It's about the student council. I don't think I should represent our class anymore. I mean, Miss Poe chose me for being honest and I've really blown that.'

Mr Trelunki smiled and sat back down. 'No, Darin. You're wrong. You do belong on the council. The fact that you are willing to step down is a sign of maturity and integrity. No one's perfect, that's for sure. But a real leader recognizes his faults and makes an effort to do better. You're doing that already, Darin.'

'But...'

Mr Trelunki shook his head. 'I've already thought about this and I want you to remain on the student council. In fact, when I talked to your class on Friday, I brought the subject up and your classmates all still want you to represent them.' Mr Trelunki stood and opened his door. 'Go on back to class, now. I'm going to have a word with Judd when he comes in. Give him a chance, Darin. When he knows adults are on to him, he straightens up real fast and can actually be a pretty nice guy.'

God Is My Best Friend

Darin walked into his classroom just as the bell rang. Classmates poured down the hall and through the door to sit down at their own desks.

Darin's stomach tightened when he saw Judd in the doorway, but when Miss Poe spoke to him, he turned and headed back to the office.

Miss Poe took attendance and lunch count. The class was saying the pledge when Judd returned, his head down. He shuffled over to his desk and sat down without a word.

'Darin,' Miss Poe said. 'You wanted to speak to the class?'

'No,' he thought. 'I don't want to. I'm being forced to.' He stood and walked to the front of the room. The class was quieter than he ever remembered them being before. His friends were staring at him. Judd was, too. Darin started to sweat.

'Go ahead, Darin,' Miss Poe said.

'Uh, my parents told me to do this,' he began. 'At first the idea made me mad because I didn't think this whole mess was really my fault.' Darin shifted from one foot to the other and forced his hands in and out of his pockets. 'But last Friday I realized that if I hadn't taken my dad's medal without permission, none of this would have happened.'

Several students started whispering to each other and stared at Judd through squinted eyes. Miss Poe had to get order before Darin could continue.

'Anyway, I want to say that I was wrong. None of this had anything to do with Judd, and I'm sorry for accusing him of something he didn't do. I hope you will all give him another chance.' Darin started to sit down, but stood once again.

There wasn't a sound in the room. Darin's knees were shaking and his pulse was pounding in his head. I'd better say this before I chicken out, he thought.

'There's something else I want to say. I thought that bringing the medal was going to make me somebody special. But when it disappeared, I realized what was really important in my life, and that is my relationship with God. You all think I go to church just because my parents make me, but that's not true. I like going to church. God is my best friend, and that's all I need to be somebody special.'

Darin sat down, keeping his eyes on his desk.

No one said anything for a few seconds.

Then Miss Poe had everyone take out their maths books and taught a lesson on multiplying fractions with uncommon denominators. When they finished, it was time for recess.

As Darin stood, Hannah reached across the aisle and touched his arm. 'That was really neat, Darin,' she said.

Darin blushed, but felt so much happiness he thought he would explode.

Andrew grabbed the soccer ball and the students headed for the field. It was Darin's day to choose one of the teams.

'Well,' he thought. 'I might as well get the ball rolling.'

'I pick Judd Becker.'

'What?' Judd held his head in his hands, took a few steps backward, and fell to the ground, pretending to faint. 'No way!' he hollered, rolling on the ground.

The other students laughed and within minutes, the class was running and working together to get the ball across the goal line.

American Words

The Purple Heart: a medal given to men and women from the United States forces who have served their country and shown great bravery.

Taking the Pledge: this is when people recite a promise in front of the American flag. Many schools in the United States begin the day by reciting this pledge.

Elementary School: a primary or junior school.

Fifth-grader: a pupil in the fifth year of elementary school.

Locker: a small cupboard where pupils keep books and other personal possessions.

Two-star General: a military commander in charge of United States forces.

Ma'am: a term of respet for women such as a teacher or your mother or older female relative.

Sir: a term of respect for men such as a teacher, your father or an older male relative.

Ball game: an expression used to describe American football, baseball or soccer.

Soccer: this word is used for what people in the United Kingdom call football.

Jump-rope: skipping rope.

Jumping-rope: skipping with a rope.

From the get-go: from the start.

Chores: household tasks.

Spelling Bee: a school spelling test.

The Ten Commandments
Exodus Chapter 20

1. You shall have no other gods before me.
2. You shall not make for yourself an idol in the form of anything in heaven or on earth or in the waters. You shall not bow down to them or worship them.
3. You shall not misuse the name of the Lord your God.
4. Remember the Sabbath day by keeping it holy. Six days you shall labor and do all your work, but the seventh day is a Sabbath to the Lord your God. On it you shall not do any work. For in six days the Lord made the heavens, earth, sea, and all that is in them, but he rested on the seventh day. Therefore the Lord blessed the Sabbath day and made it holy.

5. Honor your father and your mother, so that you may live long in the land the Lord your God is giving you.
6. You shall not murder.
7. You shall not commit adultery.
8. You shall not steal.
9. You shall not give false testimony.
10. You shall not covet.

Start collecting this series now!

Ten girls who changed the world
Corrie Ten Boom, Mary Slessor,
Joni Eareckson Tada, Isobel Kuhn,
Amy Carmichael, Elizabeth Fry, Evelyn Brand,
Gladys Aylward, Catherine Booth,
Jackie Pullinger

Ten girls who made a difference
Monica of Thagaste
Catherine Luther, Susanna Wesley,
Ann Judson, Maria Taylor,
Susannah Spurgeon, Bethan Lloyd-Jones,
Edith Schaeffer, Sabina Wurmbrand,
Ruth Bell Graham.

Ten girls who made history
Ida Scudder, Betty Green, Jeanette Li,
Mary Jane Kinnaird, Bessie Adams,
Emma Dryer, Lottie Moon,
Florence Nightingale,
Heanrietta Mears, Elisabeth Elliot.

Start collecting this series now!

Ten boys who changed the world
David Livingstone, Billy Graham,
Brother Andrew, John Newton, William Carey,
George Müller, Nicky Cruz,
Eric Liddell, Luis Palau, Adoniram Judson.

Ten boys who made a difference
Augustine of Hippo,
Jan Hus, Martin Luther,
Ulrich Zwingli, William Tyndale,
Hugh Latimer, John Calvin,
John Knox, Lord Shaftesbury,
Thomas Chalmers.

Ten boys who made history
Charles Spurgeon, Jonathan Edwards,
Samuel Rutherford, D L Moody,
Martin Lloyd Jones, A W Tozer, John Owen,
Robert Murray McCheyne, Billy Sunday,
George Whitfield.

THE CRY OF THE
WILD
BETTY SWINFORD

Scott was seized with horror. He felt like he was caught up in a whirlwind and his world was falling apart around him. Behind him, a smug-faced Ricky was smiling slyly.

The Coyote Peak Ranch is having its fair share of problems. It's not easy running a homestead at the best of times. But Scott's dog, Cadera, is causing all sorts of headaches. Has she really been killing the chickens? She is half coyote after all – a wild dog – and once wild always wild. There's nothing that can change that. But then here comes Ricky. He may be family – but he's also an enemy to Scott and to Cadera! And once an enemy always an enemy! That's the cry of the wild!

ISBN: 1-85792-8539

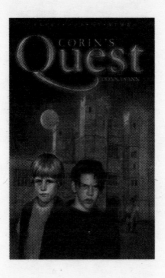

I kept the secret to myself. I hid the bundle in the kitchen under the straw where I always slept. In my heart raged a fierce battle. Oddly enough, now that I had even more reason to leave home – to find out who I really was – it seemed so wrong…'

Corin is determined to find out evil Hamo's dark secret. Aware that his life could be in danger he has to be very careful. As he starts his quest, he discovers a mystery that affects his own past and will change his life forever.

ISBN: 1-85792-2182

King Uther is dying. The Council of Elders must decide who will rule Caerleon. Why do they not see? - it must be Arthur! The nation of Caerleon is in the midst of a power vacuum. Vibiana knows who should be king... but there are others who are out to snatch power for themselves. Arthur, Cai, Vibiana and young Bem all have their part to play. Whoever finds the missing Torc is the rightful ruler. Will Arthur find the Torc and claim his rightful place as king and ruler or will the evil Morcanta's schemes succeed?

Donna Vann's emphasis on history is exemplary. Artefacts and research add another dimension to the book.

ISBN: 1-85792-8490

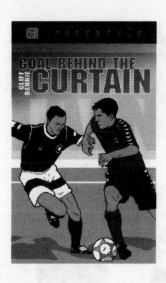

Doug Mackay has been spotted by the manager of Dalkirk Albion. It's not long before talk about the European championships arises and Doug is on the team! Word gets out that their first match is in Czechoslovakia. Doug's father asks him to meet with Christian contacts in Eastern Europe. There is a consignment of Bibles that needs delivering to a local Czechoslovakian Christian. Doug agrees to make the drop even though this could put him in danger. And with Dalkirk Albion's continued success through the European championships, Doug continues his dangerous exploits in Bible smuggling. But the biggest threat seems to be coming from his own team.

ISBN: 1-85792-6479

Look out for the sequel: Offside in Ecuatina

ISBN: 1-85792669-X

Heroes to look up to!
The Trailblazer Series

Trailblazers

Corrie ten Boom, The Watchmaker's Daughter
ISBN 1 85792 116X
Joni Eareckson Tada, Swimming against the Tide
ISBN 1 85792 833 4
Adoniram Judson, Danger on the Streets of Gold
ISBN 1 85792 6609
Isobel Kuhn, Lights in Lisuland
ISBN 1 85792 6102
C.S. Lewis - The Story Teller
ISBN 1 85792 4878
Martyn Lloyd-Jones - From Wales to Westminster
ISBN 1 85792 3499
George Müller; The Children's Champion
ISBN 1 85792 5491
John Newton, A Slave Set Free NEW
ISBN 1 85792 834 2
John Paton, A South Sea Island Rescue
ISBN 1 85792 852 0
Mary Slessor, Servant to the Slave
ISBN 1 85792 3480
Hudson Taylor, An Adventure Begins
ISBN 1 85792 4231
William Wilberforce, The Freedom Fighter
ISBN 1 85792 3715
Richard Wurmbrand, A Voice in the Dark
ISBN 1 85792 2980
Gladys Aylward, No Mountain Too High
ISBN 1 85792 5947

Torchbearers
Danger On The Hill
by C. Mackenzie

"Run, run for your lives," a young boy screamed. "Run, everybody, run. The soldiers are here."

That day on the hill is the beginning of a new and terrifying life for the three Wilson children. Margaret, Agnes and Thomas are not afraid to stand up for what they believe in, but it means that they are forced to leave their home and their parents for a life of hiding on the hills.

If you were a covenanter in the 1600s you were the enemy of the king and the authorities. But all you really wanted to do was worship God in the way he told you to in the Bible. Margaret wants to give Jesus Christ the most important place in her life, and this conviction might cost her life. There is danger on the hill for Margaret. There is danger everywhere - if you are a covenanter. The Torchbearers series are true life stories from history where Christians have suffered and died for their faith in Christ.

ISBN I 85792 7842

CHRISTIAN FOCUS

Staying faithful - Reaching out!

Christian Focus Publications publishes books for adults and children under its three main imprints: Christian Focus, Mentor and Christian Heritage. Our books reflect that God's word is reliable and Jesus is the way to know him, and live for ever with him.

Our children's publication list includes a Sunday school curriculum that covers pre-school to early teens; puzzle and activity books. We also publish personal and family devotional titles, biographies and inspirational stories that children will love.

If you are looking for quality Bible teaching for children then we have an excellent range of Bible story and age specific theological books.

From pre-school to teenage fiction, we have it covered!

Find us at our web page:
www.christianfocus.com